Acting Edition

The Ask

by Matthew Freeman

‖SAMUEL FRENCH‖

No one shall make any changes in this title(s) for the purpose of production. No part of this book may be reproduced, stored in a retrieval system, scanned, uploaded, or transmitted in any form, by any means, now known or yet to be invented, including mechanical, electronic, digital, photocopying, recording, videotaping, or otherwise, without the prior written permission of the publisher. No one shall share this title(s), or any part of this title(s), through any social media or file hosting websites.

For all inquiries regarding motion picture, television, online/digital and other media rights, please contact Concord Theatricals Corp.

MUSIC AND THIRD-PARTY MATERIALS USE NOTE

Licensees are solely responsible for obtaining formal written permission from copyright owners to use copyrighted music and/or other copyrighted third-party materials (e.g. artworks, logos) in the performance of this play and are strongly cautioned to do so. If no such permission is obtained by the licensee, then the licensee must use only original music and materials that the licensee owns and controls. Licensees are solely responsible and liable for clearances of all third-party copyrighted materials, including without limitation music, and shall indemnify the copyright owners of the play(s) and their licensing agent, Concord Theatricals Corp., against any costs, expenses, losses and liabilities arising from the use of such copyrighted third-party materials by licensees. For music, please contact the appropriate music licensing authority in your territory for the rights to any incidental music.

IMPORTANT BILLING AND CREDIT REQUIREMENTS

If you have obtained performance rights to this title, please refer to your licensing agreement for important billing and credit requirements.

THE ASK was originally co-produced by Theater Accident (Kyle Ancowitz and Matthew Freeman, Co-Founders and Artistic Directors); Rose Colored Productions LLC (Natalie Rose Ibarra, Founder) and Moira Stone; in association with The Flying Carpet Theatre Company. It premiered at The Wild Project (Ana Mari de Quesada, Producing Artistic Director; Tom Escovar, Producing Director) in New York, NY, on September 6th, 2024. The production was directed by Jessi D. Hill with scenic design by Craig Napoliello, lighting design by Daisy Long, sound design by Cody Hom, costume design by Nicole Wee, and prop design by Moira Stone. The Wardrobe Supervisor was Peter Chan. The Production Stage Manager was Karen "Curly" Schleifer, and the Assistant Stage Manager was Daren A.C. Carollo. The cast was as follows:

GRETA . . . . Betsy Aidem
TANNER . . . . .Colleen Litchfield

CHARACTERS

GRETA – (she/her) A woman in her early 70s. A liberal feminist who financially supports the causes we all care about.

TANNER – (they/them) Late 20s. Non-binary, assigned female at birth. Tanner is a Gift Planning Officer at the American Civil Liberties Union.

SETTING

Greta's study/apartment.

Tasteful art, a couch you wouldn't want to spill your coffee on, a coffee table that definitely requires coasters.

NOTE ON SET

The stage directions describe Greta's apartment as including an attached kitchenette and living room. Productions with a smaller budget may set the play in Greta's Study, but productions should include the full apartment if the budget allows.

TIME

December 2022. I won't say post-pandemic. Let's say when we all agreed to pretend the pandemic was over.

AUTHOR'S NOTE

Although this play draws heavily on my work as a fundraiser at the ACLU (American Civil Liberties Union), *The Ask* is an imagining – a work of fiction. Neither of these characters is drawn from a real person I have met or an individual I work with at the ACLU. Even the "ACLU" in the play is the subject of dramatic license: the ACLU did not experience mass layoffs in the fall/winter of 2022, for example. I do here what so many writers have done before: employ my experience of employment to talk about something that goes, I hope, beyond it.

I also hope *The Ask* displays my admiration and reverence for those that work at the ACLU – and the thousands of non-profits, big and small, that help shape our country. And I hope it shows my empathy for, and love of, those individuals that are privileged to, and tasked with, keeping the lights on at those organizations.

Among its thicket of themes, *The Ask* is about money. Money provides the outline (sometimes the chalk outline) of our lives. Even the institutions that seem to rise above the values of the marketplace wouldn't exist without money: museums, theaters, poetry foundations, human rights organizations, food banks. People work at those places, in those fields, the work they do costs money, and that money has to come from somewhere. And so, there is an exchange of energy, of earnings, of intention, and yes, a transfer from the privileged to the less so.

Money, as much as experience, seems to define this generation's divide. It has ever been thus, maybe, but I'm intrigued by the shape that divide takes today. There's something stubborn and painful about it: self-defeating, and heartbreaking, and energizing. I hope that in the *"private-made-public"* in which theater excels, we can let the stage lights illuminate how we stumble through ego, emotion, duty and doubt as we try to do good in this world.

Thank you for experiencing *The Ask*. And for the good you do in this world.

For Ellen Moncure Wong, who hired me.

(**TANNER**, *a Gift Planning Officer from the American Civil Liberties Union [ACLU], sits in Greta's Upper West Side apartment.*)

(*The apartment is laid out with an open living room and kitchen combination. There is a single hallway leading upstage left, leading to the single bedroom, single bathroom. Tasteful art and books are strewn about. This is a lived-in place, but well loved. Imagine Fran Lebowitz's apartment. Lots of books but only good ones.*)

(*On Greta's wall are fine art photographs.*[*] *Many of them of New York City, some are Greta's own work. And, in the mix, a black and white image of a dinosaur.*)

(**TANNER** *is smiling and affable but professional. They're dressed like an unthreatening activist: Brooklyn-y, the most expensive version of dressed down. Very nice sneakers.*)

(**GRETA** *is playing hostess. It comes naturally to her. She does this all the time. She's not dressed up. She just threw this on. I mean, she didn't, but she did, you know?*)

(**TANNER** *is on the couch,* **GRETA** *is in the kitchen, speaking to* **TANNER**. *Throughout*

---

[*] A license to produce *The Ask* does not include a license to publicly display any third-party or copyrighted images. Licensees must acquire rights for any copyrighted images or create their own.

the play, **GRETA** *moves throughout her apartment as she sees fit, fiddling with books, getting a snack, whatever suits her.* **TANNER** *does not leave their seat unless absolutely necessary.)*

GRETA. Do you drink coffee?

TANNER. *(It makes them jittery.)* Of course.

GRETA. I made some coffee.

TANNER. Thank you.

GRETA. Anything in it?

TANNER. Black, thanks.

GRETA. Lately I'm filling up my coffee halfway to the brim with sugar. Cuban style.

TANNER. Are you Cuban?

GRETA. No, dear I'm not Cuban. Do I look Cuban?

TANNER. I don't know.

GRETA. I'm not Cuban, for heaven's sake. I just like sugar. Where are you from?

TANNER. I live in Brooklyn.

GRETA. Where's your family from?

TANNER. I'm adopted.

GRETA. Well there you go, right there. You can't tell that by looking, can you?

TANNER. But my birth mother…

GRETA. I probably shouldn't have even asked.

(**GRETA** *puts Tanner's coffee on a coaster in front of them.)*

TANNER. It's all right. I don't mind.

GRETA. I honestly can't tell what's all right to ask.

TANNER. I asked if you were Cuban.

GRETA. Either way, the reason I drink my coffee Cuban style is because I'm officially spending half the year in Florida and I think I just picked it up, turning Floridian.

TANNER. Can I ask you a question about your photographs?

GRETA. Of course!

TANNER. Is that a Cindy Sherman?

GRETA. Good eye, it's a little print of one of the film stills. Do you know her?

TANNER. I love her.

GRETA. I love her too; I think she's a scream.

TANNER. I think she's terrifying.

GRETA. But that's what makes it funny. But you're right, scary too. Grotesque, but that always made me laugh.

TANNER. And, I'm sorry, is that a photo of a dinosaur? Because that's too funny.

GRETA. Yes it is.

TANNER. I love it.

GRETA. I'm glad! Not everyone gets it. I had this book for my nephew when he was little, it was called the *Dinosaur Dictionary*. It had a green cover, and it was filled with these photographs of models they mocked up to look like black-and-white nature photos of dinosaurs. So I took out this page with the Brontosaurus and framed it for when my nephew would visit. Now, I just call it my self-portrait. A dinosaur, surrounded by real life.

TANNER. Except for Cindy Sherman. She's not real life.

GRETA. She's a little more real than a Brontosaurus.

TANNER. That's true, that's true. And are any of the other ones yours?

GRETA. A few of my own sprinkled in, but a lot of those are on loan.

TANNER. Well, I love Cindy Sherman. And I love your work, of course. And I also have a soft spot for dinosaurs. I had a dinosaur stuffed animal. A triceratops named Sara.

GRETA. That's adorable. Well, we're going to get along just fine.

(She sips her coffee.)

That might be too sweet. I used to drink it black when I was coming up in the Village, but back then everything I did was bitter. Bitter men, bitter coffee, bitter cold winters, bitter tea. It made me feel very tough. Now, I don't know, I have a second act sweet tooth. I spent all my time when I was young fighting the world and now, I don't know, that's your job thank you very much. Now I just want a little sugar in my coffee.

TANNER. You do plenty of good in the world.

GRETA. Thank you, you're the one who does good. I just write proverbial checks.

TANNER. Well they matter.

GRETA. Yes yes you have to say that.

TANNER. Thank you for meeting me. I haven't been out the door in almost two years. It's been Zoom, only Zoom, every day Zoom.

GRETA. I know, I'm so Zoomed out.

TANNER. And you're okay with my mask off?

GRETA. I'm vaccinated to the gills. I am vaccinated to the moon.

TANNER. As long as you're comfortable.

GRETA. I am, I am. And yes no more Zoom. I'm on the board of JNF and they're still on Zoom for every meeting.

(A fake whisper.) Because everyone is so old.

TANNER. Better safe than sorry.

GRETA. Or dead, I suppose.

TANNER. Right. Better safe than dead.

GRETA. Unless, you know, I'm worth more dead than alive.

TANNER. That would make meeting rather challenging.

GRETA. Ouija Board. You could bring it right up here. I'll be haunting the place. Anything to keep them from selling it to my neighbor.

TANNER. Séances aren't in the budget.

GRETA. The halcyon days of having a budget.

TANNER. Barring that, I guess we'll have to make do with talking with the living.

GRETA. True, true. At least you get coffee out of it. Although I guess they do serve coffee at funerals too.

(They sip their coffee.)

So, Tanner, I know you're here to ask me questions, but is it okay if I ask a question first?

TANNER. Of course. What can I tell you?

GRETA. I hope this doesn't offend you.

TANNER. Nothing offends me. Or, at least, it's hard to offend me.

GRETA. Why aren't you Carol?

TANNER. *(Because half the team was let go, Carol included.)*

I know, I'm sorry I'm not Carol. Everyone loved Carol.

GRETA. Is Carol all right?

TANNER. She's at the Brennan Center now.

GRETA. Well, I wish she would have let me know. I was surprised she didn't call me to let me know.

TANNER. She didn't?

GRETA. No, nothing. Hearing from you and not Carol was my first clue.

TANNER. I'm sorry I'm not sure what happened there.

GRETA. I'm sure she has bigger fish to fry than me.

TANNER. I don't imagine that's the reason.

GRETA. Was she a part of all these layoffs?

TANNER. *(It was a terrible day. Carol cried.)*

You know, I couldn't say.

GRETA. Do you not know or are you not supposed to say?

TANNER. I don't know and if I did, I probably shouldn't say. We have an overall smaller team now, but Carol's new role, as far as I can tell, is a great one so I think it all worked out? Carol did tell me to make sure you were my first phone call when I came into this role.

GRETA. Was I the first person you called?

TANNER. *(No.)* Yes. I always listen to Carol.

GRETA. Carol's wonderful.

TANNER. Carol hired me actually.

(About the coffee.) This is good.

GRETA. It's my secret recipe: the cheap stuff. It's like wine, you know, no one can tell the difference after a certain point.

TANNER. I've read that.

GRETA. Have you?

TANNER. I think so.

GRETA. Well, have you or haven't you?

(*A moment.*)

TANNER. I don't really drink wine, honestly.

GRETA. Are you allergic?

TANNER. (*I had a serious alcohol problem.*) It's just not for me.

GRETA. You're too young to swear things off. You should try everything when you're young. You do hit a point, though, when you realize which of your friends has a problem. People start to say things like they don't want to go to a restaurant if you can't get a drink there, things like that. You notice them, functional alcoholics, because they're doing it right in front of you.

Really, it's the people with serious problems that keep them the best hidden. My nephew died of alcoholism just tragically, found in his home, and had explained the whole thing away for years as medical problems, in and out of the hospital, sickly, accident prone, whatever, but it was vodka, really, it was all just one thing, vodka, and it killed him. None of us had any idea.

People who just like to drink too much, or more than they should, those people just normalize it for themselves, it's all right out in the open. Karen drinks, John drinks, John likes his scotch, whatever. But you're too young for all that. That's for old people like me.

TANNER. You're not old.

GRETA. Oh shut up, come on. Anyway, black coffee, no alcohol, what vices do you have?

TANNER. I do buy lots of shoes.

GRETA. Oh really? Fashion.

TANNER. I line up for sneakers. I have been known to line up for a sneaker or two.

GRETA. Is that what you do with the money you raise?

TANNER. With my salary?

GRETA. I have a closetful of shoes. Do you want to look at my shoes? I don't think anything would fit you.

TANNER. I mean, it's mostly sneakers.

GRETA. Oh I don't think I have any sneakers. Anyway, I'm being too personal.

TANNER. I don't mind.

GRETA. So that's your vice. Shoes?

TANNER. It's more like a hobby than a vice. Maybe it's a vice.

GRETA. Your generation doesn't do vices, though, you're all healthy. You glow like Mormons.

TANNER. I don't think I've ever been described as glowing.

GRETA. Your skin? You glow. You're a vegan?

TANNER. No, actually, I'm not a vegan.

GRETA. Of course, you are.

TANNER. I'm not vegan.

GRETA. Vegan, no drinking, black coffee. I mean, when did we lose the libertine part of being liberal? The Right used to be the prudes, now it's our side.

TANNER. Well...our organization isn't partisan. So, I wouldn't want to say our side.

GRETA. Now it's us. Funny how that works.

TANNER. We like to say we're political but not partisan.

GRETA. Carol said that to me all the time, but I never understood it.

TANNER. No?

GRETA. What's the difference?

TANNER. I understand it's a gray area for some. I understand some of our membership is a little skeptical of...

GRETA. Of bullshit?

TANNER. I would say...

GRETA. Of creating PACs and then saying you're non-partisan?

(A moment.)

TANNER. Is that something you and Carol talked about?

GRETA. Carol agreed with me.

TANNER. I guess I could tell you what I think.

GRETA. I'm all ears.

TANNER. But what I think isn't important. I can say that the ACLU's position is that we're raising awareness about issue areas. It's Voter Education. And we'll work with whomever supports our positions, we're giving ourselves the most agility possible when it comes to advocacy and PACs provide that kind of agility. But before I get into it, I really haven't even said "thank you" yet! So I just want to say, you know, thank you. For supporting us. I intended to say that before we even started talking about all this but...

GRETA. You did actually say thank you.

TANNER. I did? I hope I did.

GRETA. You did.

TANNER. Well thank you again.

GRETA. You're welcome.

TANNER. Especially now.

GRETA. You're welcome.

TANNER. It means a lot to get a chance to say just that. To say thank you in person.

GRETA. You're welcome.

TANNER. You've really helped make our work possible.

GRETA. Thank you for the work you've historically done.

TANNER. You're welcome.

*(***TANNER*** sips their coffee.)*

So obviously you and Carol haven't met in person since…

GRETA. 2019. Right before. We actually met in the place I just sold. That was a bear.

TANNER. Your home in Florida?

GRETA. No, selling that place is a total disaster. The insurance market in Florida is now this maze, apparently. No, we met at the Maine house. I mean, I've had this place forever, and the Maine house was just getting hard for me to get to, to maintain, the size of it. Plus, the market blew up. Everyone was evacuating the cities. It wound up being a good time to sell it, but you know, it's a process, a huge process, even getting rid of something that beautiful is a nightmare. I don't want it, I say, please, take this beautiful house on the ocean and you can't imagine the questions and requests and all the things you forgot you never fixed.

TANNER. Even so.

GRETA. It's one less thing, but yes, that's where we met. Round Pond, Maine.

TANNER. So it was a summer home.

GRETA. Summer up there, winter in Florida, but I could never give up this apartment.

TANNER. It's a great place.

GRETA. It's lucky. I'm very lucky. Except for the new neighbor, she's got to be twenty-five and has a problem with everything. But that's the city. I could never give up this location.

TANNER. I was going to say.

GRETA. Where are you?

TANNER. Bushwick.

GRETA. ...I hear it's nice.

TANNER. I like it.

GRETA. I should go there. I've heard there are good restaurants.

TANNER. *(You'd hate it.)* There are. There really are.

(*Bushwick lingers in the air like a bad smell.*)

GRETA. So yes, it's been a while since I saw anyone from the ACLU.

TANNER. Yes, so I would be happy to maybe try to make up for lost time and, you were right before, I do have a few questions. They might be topics you already covered with Carol.

GRETA. You can ask. I imagine you've got a whole dossier or some notes on me or research. There was someone who came from an organization *I shall not name* – a prominent environmental organization – that went to use my bathroom and left about five pages of research about me right there on the coffee table.

TANNER. That sounds awkward.

GRETA. It was.

TANNER. Did you tell them?

GRETA. No, but it made me feel like, you know in *Mission: Impossible.* This is your mission should you choose to accept it.

TANNER. Those movies?

GRETA. The television show.

TANNER. I didn't know there was a television show.

GRETA. Well, there was. So, if I am your mission should you choose to accept it, I hope you have the good grace to leave it tucked away.

TANNER. *(I brought a file on you in my bag.)* Don't worry, I did not bring a file on you.

GRETA. All right, so you have a question.

TANNER. I guess I was just curious what first inspired you to join the ACLU. Why did you begin supporting us? Become a member? Or when did you–? Maybe you and Carol talked about this?

GRETA. That's a good question.

> *(It is a good question.* **GRETA** *tries to remember.)*

I'm trying to remember now but I think the first time I even heard about the ACLU was *Skokie*. I think there was something about an organization standing up for the principle of free speech, even for the worst speech imaginable, I know I had friends who were disgusted by it, but maybe I'm just a contrarian but I thought that was important. The idea that in order to defend speech for *some* of us we have to defend speech for *all* of us. I think back then it was more, okay I like the ACLU, I like that idea of it, but I didn't have any money back then, it was more I approved of it, I have no idea how far your records go back but I don't think I gave anything at all. I was just generally positive. Then, it was George Bush.

TANNER. 9/11.

GRETA. No, the first one. The father. The debate with, the Presidential debate with Michael Dukakis when he accused Dukakis of being a card-carrying member of the ACLU, I don't know if you remember, or no you weren't even born yet.

TANNER. I've heard about it.

GRETA. I think a lot of us were saying to ourselves "what exactly is wrong with that?" It sounded like McCarthyism or something, "have you now or have you ever been a member of the Communist Party," that kind of talk, so I got my membership card.

TANNER. That's so interesting. And where has the ACLU been on your priorities list? Do you support other organizations at a similar level?

GRETA. I support, you know, Planned Parenthood.

TANNER. Me too.

GRETA. Southern Poverty Law Center but they have some work to do, I think. They've had some issues, need to get their house in order. I'm on the board of a few small things, just when I'm asked, I used to like it but now that it's all Zoom it's a lot less rewarding. Plus, after John, there's only me keeping after everything so I have less time. But I try. City Harvest.

TANNER. Do you support candidates?

GRETA. Oh yes, but it's the worst, isn't it? I have friends that host things, and you get to meet people you see on MSNBC, but it's usually awful.

TANNER. Full dance card.

GRETA. The ACLU was the big one. As you remind me, it does go back a few years. All of that feels like a long time ago. I feel like it's a very different organization now.

TANNER. Do you think so?

GRETA. Sometimes, some of the emails I get.

TANNER. We do send a lot of them. I know it can be a lot.

GRETA. It's too much. I really don't need the paper mail. I read most of the emails. I feel like I'm reading a lot in the *Times* about layoffs, though. Is that right?

TANNER. Right, that's been out there. Yes, there's been belt-tightening.

GRETA. I think your Executive Director called it right-sizing.

TANNER. *(What an asshole.)* That's what he said.

GRETA. I think that's a terrible phrase.

TANNER. It's not my favorite.

GRETA. Was Carol right-sized?

(**TANNER** *thinks about answering.*)

You can't say.

TANNER. I just think, you know, legally I don't know what I'm supposed to talk about or not. About why someone left. The circumstances.

GRETA. Well now it sounds like Carol killed someone.

TANNER. I can, I think, confirm that she did not kill anyone.

GRETA. Safe ground there. Anyway, it seems strange that you'd come here asking about my will when you need money now.

TANNER. I don't know what you mean. I didn't come to ask about your will.

GRETA. You're in Planned Giving.

TANNER. I'm a Gift Planning Officer.

GRETA. So that's about my estate. Isn't that what Gift Planning means? Planned Giving?

TANNER. Sometimes it is. Sometimes.

GRETA. Don't you need money now?

TANNER. I mean, my role is…

GRETA. Asking about my will, I know. But, I'm probably getting you all out of order.

TANNER. No, no, it's not that, I just don't think of my role that way. I don't, well, look, I think we're all wearing a lot of hats these days, our roles are less *defined* if that's the word, and really even if I was going to ask about that, I hope that wouldn't preclude you making your annual gift or…

GRETA. I haven't decided what I'm doing yet.

TANNER. You haven't.

GRETA. Not yet, that's why we're talking. That's why I said yes to talking. You asked if I wanted to talk and that's why I said yes.

TANNER. I'm glad we're talking then.

GRETA. So before we just assume I'm writing a check…

TANNER. I didn't mean to presume or assume anything or, I hope that wasn't what I implied. I just meant that if we have one conversation that doesn't mean it's the only conversation we can ever have.

GRETA. I understand that.

TANNER. But it sounds like there's something that you want addressed?

GRETA. There is something I would like addressed. A few things, actually. If that's all right.

TANNER. Of course, fire away.

GRETA. That's the spirit. And look, Tanner, I know you can't do anything about this, but let's call this *feedback* for you to bring back with you. Getting a call from you, who I do not know, out of the blue, without any idea that I would be talking to someone else, after years of talking to one person, that's jarring. It's not, I don't think it's a...

TANNER. Not a best practice.

GRETA. It's just not very *nice*. It's not a very nice experience. It makes me feel like your predecessor was treating me a certain way because it was her job and when it was no longer her job, she didn't feel obligated to show me any grace or politeness. That makes me feel distrustful, if that's the right word.

TANNER. I understand that. I think we do try to avoid that.

GRETA. And knowing Carol, she wouldn't have treated me like that. So it makes me wonder if Carol didn't leave because she wanted to leave, or if something happened, with Carol. Which you can't speak to, but here you are, and you're just someone completely new and I feel like it's starting over from zero.

TANNER. *(I'm sure Carol would apologize for having her life upended if she could.)*

I'm sorry you feel that way. I will definitely bring that feedback back to the team.

GRETA. I hope you will. I just felt like that should be addressed. Not your fault, I know it's not your fault, but you represent the ACLU today, and so if you're the person I can tell, you get to hear it. Lucky you.

TANNER. I completely understand. I think there might be...

(Thinks better of going down that road.)

I completely understand.

GRETA. And now you want to tell me what I can do for you.

TANNER. No, I was thinking…that you're saying you don't know me, and I'm realizing, of course, you really don't. You don't know what my values are, you don't know what drives me, so that's a kind of one-sided relationship and I can see how that could be uncomfortable. So, in the spirit of transparency, maybe, to address that in the room? You should know how incredibly proud I am to work for the ACLU. How it's really an organization I feel aligned with, how it's my privilege to do this work and meet with people like you, who make this work possible.

GRETA. And you like dinosaurs.

TANNER. Yes, and that.

GRETA. Is your background law?

TANNER. No, I have a theatre degree.

GRETA. I love theatre. Do you act?

TANNER. Not as often as I'd like.

GRETA. You look like an actor.

TANNER. *(What does that mean?)* That's very…

GRETA. Did you see *Merrily* [*We Roll Along*]? With Jonathan Groff?

TANNER. With Daniel Radcliffe?

GRETA. That's the Harry Potter person?

TANNER. I haven't seen it.

GRETA. I won't even ask what you think about J. K. Rowling.

TANNER. *(Seriously?)* You probably shouldn't.

GRETA. I'm sorry, I was trying to make a joke but maybe that's not funny.

TANNER. It's fine.

GRETA. Harry Potter was good in it. It was okay.

TANNER. It's fine. Maybe we could move on.

GRETA. Right but you're not a lawyer.

TANNER. No. But, if you want to know more about me, if that would help you, I just really believe in the mission. The ACLU helps people. It stands up for people who can't stand up for themselves, it defends...

GRETA. The Constitution.

TANNER. Civil rights and civil liberties for everyone who calls this country home.

GRETA. I understand. But yes, we're both here because we believe in defending the Constitution.

TANNER. Right, that's right.

GRETA. You don't have to sell me.

TANNER. I would never try to sell you. I just want you to know who you're talking to and that I really believe in this work.

GRETA. I know it's important work. Especially after fucking Alito.

TANNER. I was going to ask how you're feeling post *Dobbs*.

GRETA. It's a nightmare. It's enraging.

TANNER. It's heartbreaking.

GRETA. So what are you all going to do about it? Is there anything we can do? Is there anything to do?

TANNER. The future looks unfortunately like a state-by-state fight. We're going to have places in the country where abortion is protected and other regions where it's almost impossible to get access to healthcare. And if the midterms told us anything, it's that when we put the question directly to voters, they choose reproductive rights. So, we're going to go hard on ballot initiatives in the states.

GRETA. And the Supreme Court. It seems like with all the conflicts of interest there's something that could be done there. Thomas is practically a January 6th co-conspirator and he's what? Just allowed to remain on the bench? His wife is a traitor. He's a traitor.

TANNER. It's frustrating.

GRETA. On Rachel Maddow, she said he could be impeached.

TANNER. I think the legal team is hesitant to take public positions against the Justices.

GRETA. Didn't you come out against Kavanaugh?

TANNER. We recommended he not be put on the bench, but it was a controversial decision that the board approved after a lot of debate. Not everyone thought it was the right thing to do, I think. So, yes, Thomas's conflicts –

GRETA. He's a traitor, his wife's a traitor.

TANNER. I don't think there's a whole lot that can be done except...

GRETA. So you're not going to do anything about them. You're the ACLU, you're supposed to have a, I don't know, strategy. An approach. To Thomas. To Alito.

TANNER. I know it's not your favorite answer, but the strategy is to continue to fight in the states, make our case, ensure that pregnant people who need abortions and access to care –

GRETA. That sounds like the plan before *Dobbs*. So, that's not very encouraging.

TANNER. It's going to be a bad time for a lot of pregnant people, but when we take our case directly to the voters, then you can see the results. Michigan, Kansas, these aren't states where we automatically win, but it drives people to the polls. We have to think long-term…

GRETA. Like a gift when I'm dead?

TANNER. I don't mean that necessarily, but…

GRETA. So what *do* you mean?

TANNER. The anti-choice movement lost for years before they were finally able to overturn *Roe*. So, we're going to have to think long-term too. Plus, *Roe* was always the floor, not the ceiling, even Ruth Bader Ginsburg thought so. So maybe this shows we need an *affirmative* right codified in the legislature.

GRETA. Do you think that's going to happen? *Congress passes a law?*

TANNER. In states we'll probably see better results first. If you're asking if we can see Congress passing a federal law this year, no, that's not going to happen. Not this year or next year or in the next four or eight years. We need to think fifty years out, we need to think about where we want to be now so we can get there, not next election cycle, but the next generation.

GRETA. Right well, I certainly hope the next generation does better than we have. And I hope that we aren't going to have to wait a half century before we get some justice, or until those fuckers die.

TANNER. So do I. So do I.

It's going to require both things, I think, giving long term and being strategic now. It's all hands on deck.

GRETA. All right.

TANNER. Did Carol ever talk with you about other ways to give? Besides writing a check? Life-income gifts? Using your IRA to make a donation?

GRETA. Is that like annuities?

TANNER. Right.

GRETA. My alma mater hounds me about those.

TANNER. I imagine.

GRETA. Because now I'm of the age.

TANNER. Do you understand how they work?

GRETA. You've come all this way to tell me how they work.

TANNER. All this way as in uptown?

GRETA. The point is, I'm happy to listen, if you want to tell me, I can't pretend to actually know.

TANNER. I'm not recommending you do anything I just think it's worth knowing how else you can make gifts to the ACLU. Food for thought.

GRETA. Again, I haven't made up my mind about anything yet.

TANNER. And we should talk about that.

GRETA. If we must, we should.

(Here comes the spiel, **TANNER** *hopes they explain this correctly.)*

TANNER. I guess for me, in my role, my responsibility, really, is to make sure that ACLU members understand the full range of options available to them. There are ways to give that can be more tax advantageous than others. You sold your house in Maine. Had you owned it for a long time?

GRETA. We bought in ninety-five.

TANNER. When you sold it, you probably had a tax bill for the capital gains from the sale of the property that year. Maybe you offset the gains in some way, I'm sure you have plenty of advice in that regard. But let's say you wanted to make a charitable gift to the ACLU and you were going to sell a piece of property in that same year. Some donors who want to make a gift in that circumstance might set up a Charitable Reminder Trust. Basically, the trust might receive the proceeds of the sale and then use those proceeds to disburse income to the donor, say five percent of the assets of the trust, valued annually, until a date certain. Most of the time the payments continue until the donor matures...

GRETA. When it matures. Or when I mature. Completely. When I can mature no further.

TANNER. I mean, depending on how you set it up.

GRETA. I don't know if I got all that, but I've already sold my house.

TANNER. I just thought, as an example.

GRETA. I don't think I followed all of that.

TANNER. Well I... I can send you some info about it.

GRETA. I don't think you need to, I've already sold my house, but if you want to email me whatever it is you just tried to explain, maybe I'll understand it better.

TANNER. All right, I understand it may not apply to you exactly, but it's an example of a way to make a gift and also receive additional retirement income.

GRETA. And people do this.

TANNER. They do.

GRETA. And that's a gift annuity.

TANNER. So, a charitable gift annuity is a lot simpler than what I just described.

GRETA. I'm so glad to hear that. How can you do this job and not drink?

TANNER. Right, I know, right?

GRETA. What's the other thing?

TANNER. A charitable gift annuity is a split-interest agreement made between a charitable organization and a donor. A donor agrees to make a charitable gift in exchange for lifetime payments. Generally, the payment rate varies based on the age of the individual making the gift. So, for example, if you were an individual at seventy years of age and created a charitable gift annuity with $100,000 today, your annuity rate would be 5.9 percent or $5,900 annually.

GRETA. That doesn't seem like a lot of money.

TANNER. The rates get higher as you get older.

GRETA. I don't plan on getting any older.

TANNER. Right but...

GRETA. Sorry don't let me derail you, I just get antsy.

TANNER. There are other ways to make it work, you could defer payments until a later date, for example. And yes, the payments are generally supplementary retirement income.

GRETA. So why would someone do this?

TANNER. Lots of reasons. Some people have appreciated securities with significant gain, so they use those to fund a gift annuity. That way you don't incur capital gains in the year the gift is made, you get a charitable deduction for the gift portion, and you get payments in exchange.

GRETA. All right, well, I don't need more retirement income. So this might not be for me.

TANNER. That makes sense.

GRETA. And wouldn't you rather I just gave the money now? I don't get why you'd prefer this?

TANNER. I wouldn't say we prefer this.

GRETA. What would you prefer?

TANNER. I don't really think of it that way.

GRETA. I don't understand.

TANNER. The best gift for you is the gift I hope you'll make. Whatever that means for you.

GRETA. That doesn't mean anything to me.

TANNER. The best gift for you means…a gift that makes financial sense, a gift that expresses your values, a gift that maybe helps make the changes you want to see in the world. This may sound corny but…I think of it as a gift that makes you happy.

GRETA. A gift that makes me happy. I see. That's a new one.

(**GRETA** *considers.*)

You know, this is all very interesting.

TANNER. I hear a "but" coming.

GRETA. But, what's the term you people have for people like me? "Lybunts?"

TANNER. (*"You people."*) I'm sorry?

GRETA. Last Year But Unfortunately Not This Year.

TANNER. I think I assumed because there was a lapse in communication, you didn't make a gift last year.

GRETA. That's not correct. It wasn't just because no one called me. I was upset. I am upset. I'm disappointed. I did not give because I did not want to give.

(*A moment.*)

Yes, you send too many emails, but I do read them. And all I'm reading is how you want money for things that have nothing to do with your mission, nothing. I even read a story about how members of your staff were calling the Constitution a white supremacist document. So, of course, I think to myself: what the heck is going on over there? And then *Dobbs*, we lose *Roe*, and you're over here playing around with trying to cancel student debt while fucking Alito is burning witches.

TANNER. I hear you.

GRETA. So you tell me I should make the best gift for me that makes me happy and I say I'm sorry, what about this situation is supposed to make me happy?

TANNER. Okay, let's take a step back, I think. This is maybe where we should have started. I think we should have maybe, maybe we should have started with my asking about this.

GRETA. I think we should have. Maybe it would have saved us both some time.

    (**GRETA** *takes out her phone.*)

Hold on just a second, let me answer my boyfriend. He's blowing up my phone. Am I keeping you? Do you have a meeting after this one?

TANNER. No, no, take your time.

GRETA. All right. Do you need more coffee?

TANNER. No, I'm just fine. Thank you so much.

GRETA. Two minutes.

    (**GRETA** *puts her phone to her ear and walks upstage into the bedroom, disappearing.*)

    (**TANNER** *takes another sip of their coffee and looks around the room.*)

*(Then, **TANNER**, much to their own surprise, bursts into tears.)*

*(It's been a hard day. It's been hard in general. **TANNER**'s feelings have terrible timing.)*

*(**GRETA** enters to find **TANNER** crying.)*

*(**TANNER** pulls it together immediately.)*

GRETA. Oh.

(She freezes.)

Are you all right?

TANNER. *(I'm absolutely fine, this didn't happen.)* Yes.

GRETA. You're okay.

TANNER. Absolutely.

GRETA. Glass of water or anything?

TANNER. No, no.

*(**TANNER** composes themselves as **GRETA** waits.)*

GRETA. Okay?

TANNER. Yes, I apologize.

GRETA. Okay. Do you need to go?

TANNER. No, really, I'm fine. Just, life.

GRETA. Yes, life. Well. Yes.

(Pause.)

Life.

(Pause.)

Well, what was causing phone commotion is Franklin picking his daughter up at the airport. He went to the wrong one. No crisis, she's fine. JFK, not LaGuardia. I don't know what that man thinks half the time. Actually, I do know. He thinks about the Mets.

TANNER. How did you meet?

GRETA. A friend introduced us. Her assessment was that he was tall enough for me. That's a ringing endorsement from her, she's not a very nice person.

TANNER. Have you been with him very long?

GRETA. Two years.

TANNER. So you met during Covid?

GRETA. We did. It was a logistical nightmare, but you know, sitting around here alone all day wasn't very good for me either. We had a Zoom date. He sent me, actually, this whole kit for how to set up the table like a restaurant and we both got delivery from the same place. It was like going out. It was cute. He's very cute.

TANNER. I love that.

GRETA. You're married.

TANNER. *(It's complicated, but sort of.)* Oh. Yeah. The ring, yes.

GRETA. Do you want my advice? Things are never fair. Fair is an illusion. Do more than your share and you'll be fine.

TANNER. *(This seems like bad advice.)* Thank you, that's good advice.

(**TANNER** *tries to get this visit back on track.*)

So, I was thinking about that old joke. You've heard that joke about if you agree with the ACLU half the time?

GRETA. Which joke is this?

TANNER. If you agree with the ACLU most of the time you should be a member. If you agree with the ACLU half the time you should be a board member.

GRETA. I think I have heard that one. I feel like that's less a joke and more of a saying.

TANNER. Either way, I think it's true. Supporting free speech, all by itself, is never going to please everyone. There are people who believe we should be free speech absolutists, but then there are those who weaponize the idea of free speech to try force a reduction in what are basically community standards, so they can use hate speech on, I don't know, Twitter without any blowback. It's got nothing to do with the Constitution, but it's framed as this free speech debate. And look at the idea that undergirded *Skokie*: defend hate speech to protect all speech. But isn't it easier for someone with privilege, who is rarely the target of hate speech, to stand up for some abstract principle? If the ACLU takes mitigating factors into account, like for example, if it doesn't represent armed protestors, then are those small carve-outs inconsistent with our mission?

I guess my point is, disagreeing with the ACLU is a pretty common experience and for good reason. I imagine there have been other times we've taken positions you haven't liked. If that's a fair assumption, what would you say is different now?

GRETA. I think what I just heard you say is different now.

TANNER. What is that?

GRETA. Trying to hold every position possible on freedom of speech. That's like holding no position at all. I thought this was an issue that the ACLU did not negotiate on. The idea that I have to say this to a member of the ACLU staff, who should have this bedrock, I don't know, faith or stubbornness about freedom of speech, it's bizarre to me. It's bizarre. I think it's this new, I don't know, it's this desire for words to "do no harm." You can't "do no harm" and have freedom of speech.

TANNER. You can acknowledge harm. You can work to reduce harm.

GRETA. Is that the ACLU's mission? To reduce harm?

TANNER. Sometimes it is.

GRETA. I don't know, I don't think so. Carol asked me to help pay for a young woman to be flown to a state where she could get an abortion and I thought, this is a good cause, and it's at least related to the mission? But these systemic goals? High-speed internet for underserved communities? How is that a Constitutional right?

TANNER. Before I answer that, is it okay if I ask a separate question?

GRETA. Go ahead.

TANNER. I guess I'm asking if you're giving less to *everyone* or only us. Because the reduction you're seeing in staffing? That's really sector-wide. There's been an overall softening everywhere and there are theories about why, some data, but I was just curious if for you it's specific or general.

GRETA. What do *you* think accounts for that?

TANNER. As far as I've heard from my colleagues, they expected some give in the budget after Trump left office. Fight's over. We all collectively took a step back, took a breath.

GRETA. You credit your layoffs to *what*? Joe Biden wins, crisis averted, people give less.

TANNER. That's right.

GRETA. Right. So bad presidents are good for business.

TANNER. I wouldn't say *business*. But yes, the Trump Bump was a real thing and now that he's out of power, we're seeing reduced revenue and membership across the sector. Especially among people in a certain demographic.

GRETA. This is where you lose me, or not just you, I know it's not you, I just think, this is the problem. The answer is, it's just how it is, it's just the weather. It's the sector. It's systemic. Everything is systemic. It removes cause and effect on the personal level. It removes the individual.

I imagine, in your life, your individuality is important to you. Asserting your identity, your uniqueness, that's been important to you. It might have even been a struggle. I don't want to assume anything, but I imagine that's true for you?

TANNER. *(Not your business, but...)* Yes, it's been a struggle.

GRETA. Right, and I'm sorry about that, but you see, I *also* want to be treated as an individual. As a woman, I mean, as a woman I've had to fight against the perception that I am a certain way, that I am defined by all these stereotypes about women.

TANNER. *(Where is this coming from?)* I get that, I do. I guess...could you tell me more about that?

GRETA. Tell you more about that. Tell you more about that.

Okay.

When we first bought the house in Florida, right before John died, I went to buy a car at a dealership. I just needed something to drive around, easy. The salesman basically ignored me until I flagged him down and asked him if he could, you know, show me a car. He asked me if I was waiting for my husband. Then, when I said, no I'm here to buy something on my own, my husband has cancer, he asked me if I might want to call a brother or someone like that. I explained that I would be fine, I would like to just look at a car.

He showed me a few cars and there was a stick shift that I liked. He told me that it was a manual and I wouldn't want it. I told him I knew how to drive stick, which you can imagine how his eyebrows went up, and then he made me *drive it front of him* before he would sell it to me. Literally said he didn't want to sell it unless he was sure I could drive it. So, I had to perform for this little man, drive a little car around the lot, to prove I could drive a car. Why I would want to buy a car I didn't know how to drive is beyond me, but there he was, watching me with his arms folded.

Anyway, after this, I told him I wanted to buy it and he sent me over to the financing desk. When I got there, I explained to the person at that desk that I no longer wanted to buy the car. I told them that clearly there was something wrong with it, because that man was so uncertain that he should sell it to me. And I left. I went home.

I got a phone call from someone at the dealership asking what happened. I explained there must be something wrong with the car, or else why wouldn't he sell it to me? Why did he make me drive it if there's nothing wrong with it? They assured me that they would happily sell me the car, and I talked them down in price, because you should *always*, and then I said I would only come back if *that man was not there when I got there.*

He was *not* there when I got there.

So, to stand here, and have you tell me that I'm just representative of some group? That maybe all *widows* are giving less right now so it doesn't have anything to do with your policies or emails? That doesn't sit well with me. To answer the question you're asking, I think:

yes, it is because of the ACLU's policies that I did not give last year. Because of my own individual assessment of where you're falling short.

TANNER. *(This has gone off the rails.)* I hear you. I...really appreciate you telling me about that. I didn't mean to, I didn't mean to... I don't think I...

GRETA. I know how important *Roe* was because I've lived in a world without it.

TANNER. I understand.

GRETA. I had an abortion when I was sixteen.

TANNER. I didn't realize that.

GRETA. I told Carol about all this. This is not in your notes somewhere?

TANNER. No, I'm sorry, it isn't.

> (**TANNER** *tries to figure out how to transition. Decides not to try.*)

I can... I can see how important this fight is to you.

GRETA. That's why I need to understand something from you. Why should I continue to invest in you if you aren't going to win? We count on you to win. Not valiantly lose. Valiantly losing is very Shakespearean but it doesn't keep fascism at bay. If you lose some things, you lose them for good. You can't just look to the future. You have to win right now.

TANNER. Well look. This is just, okay, this is from me. This isn't the official position or anything, this is just me. I think that part of the problem is that there was this sustained effort on one side to find all the weaknesses in the system and ignore civility and hold their nose to get this one thing done. There were Christians who basically hate Donald Trump who voted for him because he told them he would give them anti-*Roe* judges and that's all they cared about. Taking away reproductive rights is just more important to them than anything else, so they exacted these promises and didn't compromise on what they wanted, and they thought about it as a fight they were going to eventually win. But we, I don't know, I have friends who treated voting for Hillary Clinton like something they would only do at gunpoint because she, I don't know, gave speeches to Goldman Sachs. And I get it, but that's why the conservatives got what they wanted. They were merciless and thought *long-term*. So, I know that it's painful, this is fucking awful, excuse me...

GRETA. No, it is fucking awful.

TANNER. And...well I was going to say, "here's what we have to do next" but maybe we should just stop at "it's fucking awful" because it is. There's not a lot to say about it. It's awful. It's okay for it to feel awful. It does feel awful. You read these stories, the pregnant people who are stuck, the doctors who are afraid, people literally leaving the country, moving to states where it's legal so they can at least practice medicine, it's bad out there.

GRETA. It's bad out there, and it's going to get worse. Which is why I need to hear more than, we're going to keep fighting.

TANNER. We have to work to make it better.

GRETA. That's what I want you to do.

TANNER. And we are.

GRETA. That's where I'm not so sure. I see you working on a lot of things that you have no business working on, and then when it's the Supreme Court, where we need you, you fall short.

TANNER. Where are we losing you? I mean, high-speed internet you said?

GRETA. I'll show you.

(**GRETA** *takes out her phone again.*)

GRETA. I've got an example.

TANNER. Can I use your bathroom while you look for this?

GRETA. As long as you take your research with you.

TANNER. I promise.

GRETA. End of the hall, past the living room, on the right.

(**TANNER** *stands and heads upstage, into the hall, and out of sight.*)

(**GRETA** *pages through her phone, looking for a particular email. Then,* **GRETA** *answers her phone.*)

Hello? Are you in the car? Hello you're both on... are you both on...

(**GRETA** *pulls her legs up on the couch, comfortable in her home, just chatting as if there's no one here.*)

Hi! Did you get here safely? Is your dad apologizing? Are you apologizing? Did he apologize? I told him. I told him. I know I told him. Didn't I tell you? I told him. I told him.

(*She listens.*)

I know, I know, that's what I said. I told him. Well, you're there now. You're there now. I told him. I told him I know. I told him.

(*She listens.*)

Uh huh. Uh ha. Well, I told him. I did tell you. I wrote it down for you. I told you and I wrote it down. It was on the note. So when will you be. Are we? Aren't you? Well, I can't now. I can a little bit, not long, I'm with...

(Nodding to no one.)

If he tells you then.

> *(**TANNER** returns and makes a gesture like "I don't want to interrupt!" and **GRETA** gestures "Sit down, it's fine!" **TANNER** sits down.)*

I'm here with, yes I have someone. Yes it's in the calendar. Tanner's their name?

> *(To **TANNER** sort of, to affirm this is correct. **TANNER** nods like "You nailed it, I'm Tanner.")*

I don't know how much. We're just. Look I told him I don't know what he told you but I said JFK. I think he just. He just. He used to. All the time. All the time. Well I told him. Listen I.

> *(Listens, looks at **TANNER** like "sorry!")*

Listen I. No well of course we can go, but I think at this late date it's going to cost. I understand well we can ask. He has that Park Avenue place and I don't think he's. He's not. He's not there right now so if there's. I can text him. Not right now I have. I'm with Tanner. Yes.

> *(Listens.)*

I'll text him and ask. I'm sure he'll say yes. He's never there. I don't know where, skiing. Is there still skiing? Do people still ski with climate change? I know they do. I know. Can I. What time do you think? That doesn't give me a lot of time.

> *(Listens.)*

I don't know how much longer we'll be but it... We have plenty of time for that. And yes, you have his number if you want to call him yourself. And doesn't Sarah basically own that hotel? Not own but you know what I mean. I'm sure there are lots of places to stay.

(Listens.)

I wish I could but this place is. You know it's not set up for. Yes. I'll call.

(Listens.)

It's been great, it's been a great conversation but I'm being rude. I'm being. I should go. Okay bye sweetheart. Tell him. I told him. I told him! I told him. I told you. I told him. I told him. You believe me don't you? You know I told him. Okay, I told him JFK. I'm sure. I wrote it down. Have a good drive. See you tonight. Goodbye. Bye! Bye!

(She hangs up.)

I may have told him LaGuardia.

TANNER. Everything okay? I don't mean to take up your whole afternoon.

GRETA. Franklin's daughter was supposed to stay with some friends in Murray Hill and one of them has Covid so they're scrambling to find her a place. She's seeing some shows so we'd rather she was in midtown, just easier, but you know, last minute hotels. I have a friend who's in Oslo and he has a place on Park that is most of the time empty, so I'll see if she can stay there.

TANNER. I hope you get it sorted.

GRETA. Everything gets sorted, doesn't it? Things have a way of working out. They just do.

> **(TANNER** *has not drawn that conclusion from life.)*

All right, I found the email I wanted to show you. Here. The ACLU's plan to eliminate student debt. Working with our coalition partners, the ACLU will sustain and support efforts to encourage President Biden to eliminate student debt. Yadda, yadda, yadda the disparities in student debt forgiveness make it a key part of achieving racial equity. You've seen this. I read this and I could not believe it. I could not believe it.

TANNER. As a person with student loans, I'm pretty happy about it.

GRETA. I have so many problems with this. For starters, what does this have to do with the Constitution?

TANNER. I think there's a…

GRETA. The answer is it has nothing to do with the Constitution. It's a progressive wish-list item. There are people that think student debt cancellation is actually *unconstitutional*. And how does one even do this fairly. Who gets their loan forgiven? Do you know what mission creep is?

TANNER. I do, yes.

GRETA. How is this not mission creep?

TANNER. I think it depends on how you see the mission.

GRETA. How is that even something up for debate?

TANNER. Our brand is debate!

GRETA. First of all, brand? You're not Maybelline, you're the ACLU. Second, no, your role is to stand up for the law. To advocate for civil liberties. To defend the Constitution. That's why I support the ACLU. Because it is, or it was, sane. You knew that if there was someone trying to ban a book or deny a woman's right to choose or jail a protestor, the ACLU would step in. This is, I don't even know. Postal banking. You want to spend dollars on postal banking?

TANNER. It's about access to financial resources.

GRETA. Again. Again. Financial resources. Economic justice. You're not supposed to be behaving like a wing of the Democratic Party.

TANNER. We sue the Democrats. We definitely sue the Democrats.

GRETA. I just don't understand what this has to do with the Constitution. I'm willing to have it explained to me. I am willing to hear you out. But I have to say, I'm troubled by this trend. Your emails sound like a teenager complaining about their parents. I saw a Tweet that said, "We won't put up with this bullshit!" I thought you all went to Princeton!

  (Pause.)

So, the floor is yours if you want it. I know you aren't to blame for all this, but you're the one who's here so if you have any answers for me, I'm all ears.

TANNER. Okay.

  (How to answer?)

I'm.

  *(**TANNER** thinks.)*

So.

  *(**TANNER** decides to maybe try to really explain this.)*

You just said that things have a way of working out.

  *(**TANNER** steps out onto the thin ice of explaining privilege.)*

I get why you said that. I think there's truth to that idea. My brother used to say that to me all the time and I think, I mean, I understand why it's an appealing idea. Have faith, things will work out.

Working at the ACLU though, talking with the attorneys and the community organizers, it's pretty clear why sometimes things work out, and sometimes they don't. Every city, every state, every community, is held together by policies, decisions, forces, that are meant to produce certain outcomes for the people that live there. Red-lining, over-policing, how drugs are classified, these all create different outcomes. Those outcomes are not evenly distributed, they're not equitable. But they're disguised, in a way. To most people these forces are basically invisible. Things look like they just happen, but they don't.

And I say sometimes because not every policy was intended to create a disparate outcome, that's just been the effect. For example, some software for quoting an insurance rate to an applicant will produce less favorable interest rates for Black applicants than white applicants. Interest rates have a real impact over time, especially if you're not an already wealthy person. Or if your family isn't rich. It's hard to get ahead or save money as easily. And it's based on biased data dumped into a machine.

I'm not explaining this very well.

These forces, these policies, impact our access. Access to neighborhoods, to justice, to opportunities. And access impacts our rights. A right without access doesn't really exist. Voting rights are a perfect example. If you make polling places difficult to find, limit their hours, prosecute people who fill out forms incorrectly, or require people to take time off of work to vote? The right becomes difficult to access. It becomes abstract, it exists in name only.

So, these goals, these advocacy goals, they're about the real world and how it works. Principles are important, critically important, but if you create equal opportunity employment standards, and then you require anyone who wants a job to apply for it online? Without high-speed internet everywhere, those opportunities aren't real for some people.

So, equitable outcomes have real world impacts on access to rights, to full participation in society, and I think that matters. I think that's worthy of our time, our resources, and it makes a real difference for real people.

(**GRETA** *considers this.*)

GRETA. I appreciate that perspective. I do.

(*Pause.*)

It actually sort of confirms my fears.

TANNER. How?

GRETA. Replace what you just said with hunger.

TANNER. Okay.

GRETA. Some people don't have enough to eat. If someone can't eat, if they're starving? They can't protest. They can't vote. Can they?

TANNER. Actually, I think there are plenty of people experiencing food insecurity who can and do participate in the political process.

GRETA. People with student debt can vote, can't they?

TANNER. They can vote.

GRETA. Okay just...what I'm saying is that almost anything under the sun can be traced back to "access to rights" if you use the broadest definition.

TANNER. I don't think I'm using the broadest definition.

GRETA. If someone can't eat, if they're starving even, they can't go to a polling place or a protest. So is it the ACLU's job to feed people? To give them access to their rights? Or is it the ACLU's job to make sure our Constitutional rights exist and let organizations who deal with things like starvation or internet or financial literacy deal with those things. Don't try to be everything to everyone.

TANNER. I think we're being more targeted than that, but I hear what you're saying.

GRETA. You see my issue here. My concern.

TANNER. I think, okay, I think financial literacy and access to wealth aren't actually related. But, setting that aside, I think we're trying to listen to our coalition partners, those other organizations you're talking about, and asking how our resources can be put to use to advance equity goals nationwide. Just like you're saying, there are other organizations that do these things, so we don't have to lead in order to show them our support.

GRETA. That's not how this is presented. This is presented as student debt forgiveness as an ACLU priority.

TANNER. I understand, I see how it's confusing.

GRETA. Do people on the ACLU staff really believe the Constitution is a white supremacist document? That seems like Planned Parenthood believing that life begins at conception.

TANNER. I'm. I know the article you're referring to.

(Carefully.) That article was, I would say, cherry picking internal conversations that were never meant to be, you know, official positions.

GRETA. You can see how distressing that is to read.

TANNER. I'm not asking this to punt or anything but did you and Carol talk about this before she left?

GRETA. Carol's not here.

TANNER. I know.

GRETA. You're not answering my question.

TANNER. It's pretty clear that white supremacy is a huge part of the whole American project, you can't look into any aspect of our history without finding it, the Constitution included.

GRETA. You work for the ACLU.

TANNER. I do, that's why I'm here.

GRETA. Do you think of the ACLU as patriotic?

TANNER. Patriotic? I don't know.

GRETA. We, the People, in order to form a more perfect union.

TANNER. But those people were not *We* at the time. When that document was written...

GRETA. That document!

TANNER. When the *Constitution* was written, neither of us would have been allowed to form anything. We couldn't own property. We couldn't vote.

GRETA. But now we can. Because someone believed that the rights written down in the Constitution should apply to everyone and fought for that idea.

TANNER. I agree with you. I agree that there's been progress. That's the hopeful part. The real mission isn't just holding rights and securing them for the few but ensuring that the Constitution's protections exist for everyone.

GRETA. How is that white supremacist?

TANNER. Expanding rights?

GRETA. If the Constitution is white supremacist, why would anyone want to make sure it protects more people?

TANNER. I think it depends on the context.

(**GRETA** *does not respond well to the word
"context."*)

What I understand is that some of my colleagues want
to acknowledge where we *started* as a country, so we
know how far we've come. If you acknowledge that
the Constitution didn't outlaw slavery, and that many
signers of the Declaration of Independence were slave
owners, and that they expressly removed condemnation
of slavery? If you look at that and acknowledge it, then
you can move forward without mythology. You can say
"This is missing, how do we change that?" You can't
cure your cancer if you don't admit you have it. If you
don't diagnose it.

GRETA. You can't cure cancer at all. There is no cure
for cancer. And I don't know what's so bad about
mythology? We need some mythology.

TANNER. Okay.

(*A decision to be personal.*)

When I was in Texas last year, someone followed me
into a Walmart bathroom because they thought I was
going into the wrong one. They had been so convinced
that someone who looks like me has to be watched like
a hawk, lest I pee in the wrong place and destroy the
Republic. That is not going to be true forever. That is
not going to be true for people who are growing up
now, I hope. But if I pretend that right now is fine and
that attitude doesn't exist, I can't fight it. That's all that
I think is going on. Naming what's true.

GRETA. I'm sorry. I know what you think you're saying, but
to a lot of folks, you're undermining the whole point
of your organization. It's just a bad look. You sound
entirely captured by the far left, all the emails, all the
issues, you sound even too left for the Democrats. You
sound partisan. When you sound this partisan, you

lose credibility. When you lose credibility, people stop listening. When people stop listening, you lose power.

TANNER. It's a challenge. It's a constant challenge. I hear you. I hear you.

GRETA. Well that's good to know. I feel very heard.

> *(Trying to steer this back towards making The Ask.)*

TANNER. I don't know if I've said anything to you that actually made you change your mind, but it's a conversation. I hope we can keep having that conversation.

GRETA. We'll see.

TANNER. I'm not here to debate you. I know everything you're saying is coming from a place of wanting to help. I just, it's...

> *(Pause.)*

It's...it's not about me, at all, you know? I'm not...think of me as *not here*. I'm *not here*, if you want to think about it that way.

GRETA. I don't like that. "I'm not here."

TANNER. I'm here on behalf of the people...

GRETA. You are here.

TANNER. ...who go out there and sue the people we want to sue, who stand up for our clients. So what I think, my story...

GRETA. I know you're working, I know, but you can just say what you think. I'd like you to just say what you think. You are here.

TANNER. *(Barreling ahead.)* So. So. So. I know you get a lot of texts, so many emails, I get them too, I mean, it's a lot, and they sound like Fuck Republicans or whatever, they sound left to you, or whatever, it sounds partisan to your ear. But there are people out there who respond to those texts and emails. Young people who, you know, need to be communicated with in a different way. Maybe *you* don't, maybe *you* don't need something to retweet, but if we want to reach those members, we can't sound Ivory Tower.

GRETA. You mean educated?

TANNER. We need to reach people where they are, the next generation, new members. Who need irreverence, who are very activated by the personal, the immediate, who need...

GRETA. I think eventually, if you cater to that group enough, it will change what you do. It already has. And if you think that generation is going to be as generous as the people who have historically supported you, you're out of your mind.

TANNER. I am definitely armed with that feedback when I get back to the office.

> *(If there's coffee left in the cup,* **TANNER** *finishes it.)*

That all being said, I do hope you'll consider supporting us again.

> *(Pause for a response that doesn't materialize. And so...onward.)*

If you'll forgive me, I wouldn't ask if I didn't hear all this and think that you'd like to support us. I feel like everything I'm hearing you say. You just. You really care about the ACLU. You care about what we do. You've cared for a very long time.

> *(***TANNER***'s wind up.)*

If I can just reflect back to you what I think I heard today, I think I heard that you care quite a lot for broad speech protections, for abortion rights, for the environment – which I will tell you, a free press and the right to protest goes a long way to changing how the public perceives the climate crisis. I hear that you read all of our emails, that you met with Carol for years, that you've given generously to us, that we're your top priority. I hear that you decided not to give last year so that someone would really hear what your concerns are, and I hope you can tell, you're heard, you matter to us. You're really a part of the family. So if there's some estrangement, obviously, we want to address it, so we can continue forward and advance all of our goals.

GRETA. Okay.

TANNER. So I guess what I'd hope you would consider...

GRETA. *(Cutting to the chase.)* You're already in my will.

> *(A moment.)*

When John died I updated my will. And I guess I could update it and take you out, but I probably won't because it's a hassle. So Mazel Tov, you will get money when I die.

TANNER. That's wonderful. Or, I don't mean, what I mean is thank you.

GRETA. Anyway, you're already in there. John died, my nephew died, my sister gets something and then you and a few others.

TANNER. There's a legacy society, we have events.

GRETA. Please don't invite me to any more events. I won't go to them.

TANNER. All right. Thank you. That's a really meaningful gift.

GRETA. All right. Is that all for today?

TANNER. Well I was hoping we could have the dreaded "will you support us at this level" conversation. Because, obviously, last year you decided not to give and this year we're seeing, as you saw...

GRETA. Layoffs, you need money. I have steeled myself.

TANNER. Right, there has been some, as I said, it's maybe a difficult time, but I'm going to ask you for an amount that maybe is higher than you've been asked for before. So just, I invite you to think about it before you answer right away. Because if it were possible to step up at this level right now, it would make a significant difference. A critical difference.

(The Ask.)

Would you consider supporting the ACLU at the $500,000 level this year?

(There is a long moment of tension.)

*(**TANNER** knows not to speak before the donor.)*

(It's in all the books.)

*(**GRETA** seems as if she's frozen but she's thinking this over.)*

GRETA. It's not impossible.

(She considers.)

I'm just surprised.

(She reconsiders.)

It's not impossible.

TANNER. It's a lot to consider.

GRETA. It wouldn't have been possible before –

*(**GRETA** composes herself.)*

GRETA. I'm going to say this. I'm going to start with it's not impossible.

TANNER. Thank you for really giving this some thought.

GRETA. I'm going to say that I just paid down a pledge last year to my alma mater so that's off my plate. I have to say if I did even consider making a gift of that size, I wouldn't want it to just wind up as covering overhead.

TANNER. That's something we could talk about.

GRETA. Your general operating costs. That's really something for you to figure out. I'm not interested in just filling in a gap in your budget that maybe you could make up some other way.

(Negotiating.) What if it were a pledge?

TANNER. Would that make it a lighter lift?

GRETA. I imagine you'd prefer it all as general operating, all this year.

TANNER. If that would be a strain on you, if that doesn't inspire you, then I mean, that doesn't sound like it would make sense for you.

GRETA. So you don't care how much, or when it comes in, you have nothing you'd like me to take into account.

TANNER. It's not that, it's more, like I said, this should feel like the best gift for you.

(**GRETA** *moves around her apartment, to help herself think.)*

GRETA. A gift that makes me happy. I'd have to talk to a few people. I'm not saying yes, I'm not saying no. Obviously with *Dobbs*, I'd consider making it all or in part only to reproductive rights.

TANNER. That's certainly...

GRETA. If I gave it to the cee, the...

TANNER. To the c3?[*]

GRETA. Could you use it?

TANNER. Yes.

GRETA. I know that you can't lobby with it, you can't buy ads with it.

TANNER. That's right we couldn't use it for lobbying or political advocacy but if tax deductibility is important for you.

GRETA. I understand.

(**GRETA** *isn't sure about this.*)

My first thought is that if I made that level of commitment, I'd prefer it be directed only to reproductive rights.

TANNER. *(This is not ideal.)* It can be restricted to repro if that's your priority. I feel like we've talked about other priorities too.

GRETA. I think.

(She sits and reposition herself.)

(It's time to level with **TANNER.***)*

GRETA. If I'm honest with myself, I think what I'd need is not *just* to restrict the gift to abortion rights. What we've talked about today, what I hope you heard, what you told me you heard, is that we've really lost our way. There are just too many groups that you're trying to serve and please, too many identity groups that seem to have, I don't know, become influential. There's a lot of time spent on economics and healing the world and solving injustice. It's diffuse, it's, it's idealistic, it is, but it's not effective. It's not the ACLU. If the ACLU is going to continue to receive my support, especially half a million dollars, I'm sorry I'm going to need confidence

---

[*] **A 501(c)3: a non-profit organization.**

that I'm not going to be seeing emails about the internet and student loans and, as you said, Fuck Republicans. Enough with all things to all people. I want to see First Amendment, like I said, I want to see you standing up against prejudice. You're suing people over who can make a cake in Colorado and you're policing language, who can say what, that's the opposite of freedom of speech, as far as I'm concerned. So, I need to see the ACLU get back to basics, protecting free speech on college campuses for example, and a little less of this social justice stuff.

(**TANNER** *doesn't respond.*)

I realize you're not the person who makes those decisions.

TANNER. I'm afraid I'm not.

GRETA. But if I'm going to commit to this gift, I'm afraid that matters to me. I mean, even to hear *you* say that you understand why this needs to change. That would go a long way with me.

(**TANNER** *thinks about this.*)

I mean, you can see my point, I think you do. You said you heard me. I don't know, maybe I should just talk to someone else?

TANNER. I think we can, I think we could absolutely structure a gift that states your values, restricts to abortion rights.

GRETA. But here's the thing. *"Pregnant people."*

TANNER. To protect pregnant people's rights, yes.

GRETA. No, you said that before. "Pregnant people." We were talking about abortion, and you said "pregnant people." I've seen that all over your literature. "Pregnant people," gender justice. I think you can understand my hesitation to make a gift of this size to an organization that can't even use the word "women." Woman.

(**TANNER** *tries to hide discomfort. They think they do it admirably.*)

I am not trying to be insensitive, but you have to understand, I have fought for women's rights my whole life. My series, my photos, *women's* rights. It was important to John, too, women's rights. I understand that there are other rights that exist, other groups, but LGBTQ+ etc. groups have lots of advocates. They have advocates at the ACLU. Where are our advocates? Where did they go?

TANNER. *(Oh fuck.)* It's not a zero-sum game. LGBTQ rights, the rights of femme people, queer people, pregnant people, they're connected…

GRETA. Right there. Right there. You didn't say women. Why didn't you say women?

(**TANNER** *doesn't respond.*)

Tanner, I am not saying "no" to you. I can't imagine I'm the only person who feels this way. Someone else has had to have said this to you. Hasn't anyone else said this to you?

TANNER. I hear you.

GRETA. I just don't think you *do.*

You're asking me to support an organization that I have loved, that I have *loved*, that I have supported for decades, and I tell you how unhappy I am, how disappointed, and you ask me for five times the amount that I've ever given? I'm not saying no, but have you done this for very long? You have a theatre degree? Are you also doing that? Maybe this isn't for you.

TANNER. I'm sorry you feel that way.

GRETA. That's not fair maybe. Maybe that's not fair.

TANNER. You have the right to whatever you feel. You do.

*(**TANNER** is on their back foot but tries to rally.)*

I hope that how I'm handling this, if it's not satisfactory for you, won't stop you from supporting a really worthy cause. There are people out there right now who have to cross state lines in order to access abortion care, even some prenatal care, because the clinics that can help them have been destroyed by anti-choice activists. Those people need your help. It's not me, I'm not asking you to help *me*, I'm asking you to help *them*.

GRETA. Again, you didn't say women. You didn't say *women*. I don't understand why you can't say women. Aren't most of your donors women? Isn't your board president a woman? Aren't almost all of the people who just lost the right to control their own bodies, women?

*(This is important to **GRETA**.)*

I know, I know you aren't going to be able to commit to me, right here, that you personally are going to change how far away the ACLU has gone from its mission. But if I do give this gift, then I'll need some assurances along the way, and that starts here I'm afraid. Because you're here, you're the one here, and I get the impression you're an honest person. So if you could say to me, right now, that you will take this all to heart, and help me make a gift that starts to make the ACLU live up to its own values, then we can talk.

*(**TANNER** takes this in.)*

Otherwise, it's when I die. Maybe.

*(**GRETA** doesn't realize her arms are folded.)*

TANNER. *(What does she expect me to say?)* I really appreciate us having this conversation.

(Does she think I run the whole organization?)

I think maybe I'm struggling with the outcome you're looking for. I don't know if I can make a commitment that the ACLU is always going to do things you agree with if you make this gift. I wouldn't want to say that to you. I don't think that would be honest.

> *(Should I defend using inclusive language? That'll just make this worse. Let's try:)*

And when I say p—

> *(Focus on the goal.)*

It seems as if what inspires you most is access to reproductive care. If that's your priority, it's ours too, so if you have the ability to make a gift at that level to further that cause, there's really no better time to make that gift than right now. The fight is happening right now.

> **(TANNER** *rises to leave.)*

But look, I never expected that I would come here and ask you for such an increase, especially after this visit, and leave this afternoon with an automatic yes. I knew you'd have to think about it. Maybe we can't figure that out today. Maybe we need to think about it, give it time to breathe, I can send you some ideas of how we might design a gift plan that captures everything we've talked about today.

GRETA. Tanner, I've asked you *directly* if you can make a commitment to me. A personal one. I can give you a yes right now if I know there's one person over there, you, that is my advocate. I think that's what I'm looking for here. That's why it troubles me that you use the language you do.

TANNER. I use inclusive language.

GRETA. Pregnant people.

TANNER. That includes anyone who might need care.

GRETA. I don't know how I can be expected to support an organization that has no interest in the rights of people like me.

> (**GRETA**'s *located her actual issue.*)

I think that's what it comes down to. Many women have fought for all these rights and now we have to share the room with men, I'm sorry, we do. When you say "pregnant people" you mean men who can get pregnant. I'm not saying transgender men aren't men. They are. Fine, they are. If you say so, they are men. But to have to put the word woman aside to make more room for men, even now, when we lose *Roe*, can't you understand what that feels like?

TANNER. To be marginalized.

GRETA. Yes. To be marginalized.

TANNER. Yes, I can understand what that feels like.

> (*A pregnant pause.*)

Apatosaurus.

GRETA. I'm sorry?

TANNER. You said Brontosaurus. Your photo. It's an Apatosaurus. They changed the name. Whoever decides. That's what it's called now. New evidence.

GRETA. I know. But. Old habits.

TANNER. Right.

> (*Pause.*)

I'm sorry.

> (*Pause.*)

What do you want me to say?

GRETA. I mean, I think what it comes down to? Right now? For me, is hearing you say the word *woman*. Maybe you can't promise me everything, and yes, after that, we can talk about gift agreements, whatever you like. I just want to hear some common sense.

(*Common sense, that's all* **GRETA** *wants.*)

I'd like you to say the word "woman."

(*Maybe if* **GRETA** *can get this word out of* **TANNER***'s mouth the world will feel rational again.*)

I don't think that's too big of an ask.

(**TANNER** *stares at the word, floating in front of them, in space.*)

TANNER. Woman.

(*Blackout.*)

9 780573 711626